The Wobbly To

The Wobbly Tooth

by Nancy Evans Cooney

illustrated by Marylin Hafner

G. P. Putnam's Sons · New York

Published simultaneously in Canada by General Publishing Co. Limited, Toronto.
Printed in the United States of America.
Library of Congress Cataloging in Publication Data
Cooney, Nancy Evans. The wobbly tooth.
Summary: Elizabeth Ann tries very hard to lose a wobbly tooth.
1. Teeth — Fiction I. Hafner, Marylin. II. Title.
PZ7.C7843 Wo [E] 77-14943
ISBN 0-399-20615-9
ISBN 0-399-20776-7 pbk.
First paperback edition published in 1981.
Fourth impression.

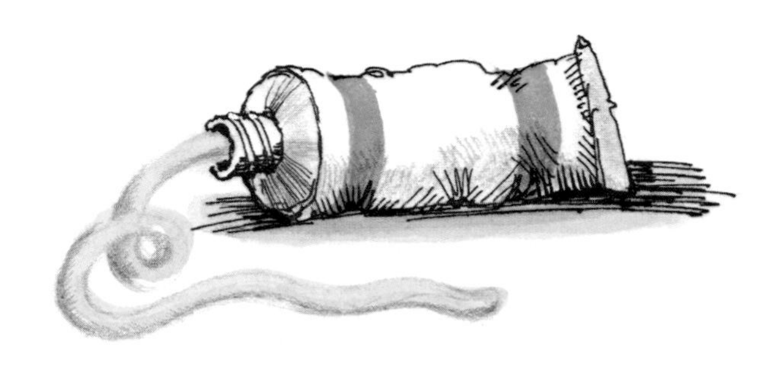

To Jimmy, Carolyn, Christine, and Mark
—N.E.C.

For Aileen and Margaret
—M.H.

Elizabeth Ann had a wobbly tooth. But this wobbly tooth was different. This tooth was stubborn.

It *wouldn't* come out.

Elizabeth Ann's mother said not to worry. "That tooth just isn't ready to come out yet."

But that wobbly tooth bothered

Elizabeth Ann. She decided to get rid of it.

She tried jiggling the tooth with her fingers.

But it wouldn't come out.

She tried brushing with her daddy's electric toothbrush, with the extra-stiff bristles, until her arm shook.

But it wouldn't come out.

She tried hopping up and down with stiff knees.

But it wouldn't come out.

She tried turning cartwheels across the front lawn until she got dizzy.

But it wouldn't come out.

She even tried munching on her favorite chewy, nutty, nougat-and-caramel covered-with-chocolate bar.

But it wouldn't come out.

Elizabeth Ann sat glumly on her doorstep. She had run out of ideas.

Maybe her mother was right. That tooth just wasn't ready to come out.

So Elizabeth Ann decided that she would forget all about that old wobbly tooth.

She took her best book about wild horses from the corner bookshelf near her bed and started to read. But her tongue kept remembering that wobbly tooth, and kept sneaking over to touch it. She put the book away.

She chewed some bubble gum—only in the left side of her mouth, of course—as she climbed on the old jungle gym in the backyard. But she couldn't blow anything better than a lopsided Ping-Pong-ball-sized bubble. She threw the gum in the garbage can.

She sang her private little "tra-la-la" song as she roller-skated up and down her front sidewalk. The "tras" were just fine, but the "la-la-las" kept bumping into that wobbly tooth.

Elizabeth Ann put her skates back in the hall closet.

She sighed.

She couldn't forget that tooth no matter how hard she tried!

So when Jane came over to ask her to join in a baseball game, Elizabeth Ann said, "Great!"

She liked playing baseball with her friends. She liked the smell of her leather glove. She liked the lovely *thud* that meant she had made a good catch.

And she especially liked to hit the ball so hard that it flew over the hedge into the neighbor's yard.

It was a tough game. First one team scored, then the other.

Elizabeth Ann was so busy trying to help her team that she even forgot all about forgetting.

In the first inning she just missed tagging a runner out at third base. Later she hit a fly ball right to the center fielder.

By the last inning her team was still behind by one run. Surely she could score to tie the game!

She stepped up to the plate and grasped the bat.

The first pitch whizzed by before she could swing. When the next pitch came, she was ready.

Crack went the ball when she hit it. It sailed past first base. So did Elizabeth Ann.

On the ball flew. On ran Elizabeth Ann.

She touched second base and then third. She headed toward home plate. Elizabeth Ann saw the ball coming.

She raced faster and faster and finally slid into home plate in a cloud of dust.

But the ball got there first.

She was out!

Elizabeth Ann sat panting and dusty and feeling very disappointed. What a day! Nothing seemed to go right and now she couldn't even get her run.

She grinned weakly at her teammates. "I tried," she said.

But Jane cried, "Look!"

Elizabeth Ann looked at everyone else, but they were looking at her.

"Elizabeth Ann has lost a tooth!"

Elizabeth Ann's tongue flitted over to feel her tooth. There was nothing but a hole instead. That wobbly tooth was gone!

She smiled.

It must have been ready to come out at last.